MAY I CALL YOU MISTRESS?

RUBY SCOTT

Ruby Scott

www.rubyscott.com

A THOUGHT...

"Ignore what a person desires, and you ignore the very source of their power."

- Walter Lippmann

CHAPTER ONE

"I wouldn't ask unless I had to. You know that, don't you?"
Matt dissolved into another fit of coughing, and Abby gave
an involuntary shudder as the sound of mucus rattled
through the phone.

"I know. I know," she repeated, grabbing an envelope
from the pile of unopened bills which sat on the top of the
microwave. A sticky residue caught her hand as she reached
for the pen. "Oh, for fuck's sake." Still holding the pen,
Abby lifted the side of her hand to her mouth and licked.
Yup, it was definitely honey. That was a relief. Letting out a
long sigh, she tapped out an impatient rhythm with the pen
nib on the paper, waiting for Matt's coughing to subside.
When it did, she wasted no time.

"Right. What's the address?"

"It's Mill Farm Road, Aberdour. Well, it's not *in* Aberdour. It's about five minutes outside of the village," Matt
said in a thin wheeze. "I'll WhatsApp you the directions
and coordinates. Just follow the road to the bend. You can't
miss it."

"Mm." *Like the last Glencoe shoot,* she thought, but

decided not to vocalise the cynicism she held towards her friend's navigational prowess, or rather lack of it. On that trip, Betty, her battered, brown Renault Clio, had to be abandoned halfway up a sheep track. Mind you, being rescued by the rather luscious Lisa, a smallholder with a throbbing quad bike, had given the day a welcome upturn.

"I've let Victoria know you'll be there by nine, ready to start."

"What you've already—"

"Abby, you're a fucking star. You know that. Right?"

Abby rolled her eyes at Matt's stock question. It'd taken a few months after they'd first met to realise it wasn't rhetorical, because frustratingly, if she didn't respond with immediate agreement, then he'd just keep asking. The balance between fondness and downright irritation with him was always in equal measure.

"Yes, Matt, I know that. Send me across the job sheet and the address and I'll get it done, but you owe me. Big time." Abby was pretty sure Matt spluttered some more thanks, but she didn't hang on the line any longer than she had to. Ill people were never really her thing.

Hanging up, she leant into her kit bag and pulled out a bottle of sanitiser. The clear blob hit her palm with a reassuring *plop* and she worked it over her skin, as though Matt's virus could have seeped through the phone line.

The screen lit up with directions for tomorrow. One tap later and the full spec appeared.

Client: Victoria Fraser.

Address: Tigh Na Dànachd, Mill Farm Road, Aberdour.

Details: Product shoot for website. Adult themed.

Abby's eyebrows raised. This was a little different from her bread-and-butter wedding shoot. Intrigued, she read on.

There were approximately twenty new products being added to an existing online retail business. Her fingers sped across the MacBook keyboard, typing the site address, wetforwomen.co.

Abby came face to boobs with a tanned, well-endowed pair of—yup, given the proximity and placement of their hands, it was a safe bet they were lesbians.

Running her finger over the trackpad, Abby decided the favour she was doing Matt might not be such a hardship after all. Besides, if she wasn't covering Matt's shoot, she'd be spending the day editing images of couples cooing over each other, dripping in love.

Eurgh!

The poor saps had no idea how fast it would all come tumbling down once the shine had worn off. They'd wake up one morning to the realisation that they had already peaked, leaving them warped together in a sad spiral of descent for the rest of their days. At least that was the matter-of-fact reason Katie offered for the end of *their* marriage. It happened over porridge one morning, with such quick efficiency, Abby's bowl was still warm when the door slammed closed for the last time. That had been eighteen months ago, and Abby still couldn't reconcile Katie's vision of bleak oblivion with her own excited anticipation for the holiday they'd booked to Disney. To this day, she still hadn't ridden the Seven Dwarfs Mine Train, plus she'd never been able to face oats again.

Wetforwomen.co offered a line of lube that came in a variety of flavours, including "Stuffed Jalapeño." Stuffed with what? She mused, before being distracted by the sleek designer dildo range. They were USB chargeable. The sort of toys that didn't need batteries, or a motivational team talk before the big game...the sort Abby aspired to own.

Perhaps tomorrow's shoot was for a new range? Abby checked her watch. In exactly eleven hours, she'd have her answer. There might even be a chance that she'd be rewarded with a free sample, or two. God knows she could do with an upgrade. Not a sudden jump to first or even business class, but making it out of cargo would be a start.

———

"Where the f—," Abby threw the soft velvet cushion against the sofa in frustration. The only upside to shooting weddings every week was the standard gear never varied and she could gather everything she needed blindfolded, inside of five minutes. Crucially, that meant an additional half an hour in bed. But this morning when the alarm, she could have sworn she'd set, didn't go off—damn Alexa, and Bezos—her swanky Bluetooth speedlights, which she never used, were nowhere to be found. It wasn't until the precariously balanced box labelled "Cables and Shit" toppled and spewed, did she see them cowering in the corner of the walk-in cupboard, aka the darkroom. Not that she'd developed a single image behind that door, but so named because she'd never gotten around to fitting a light.

Ten minutes later, she was off. Betty squealed in anguish as Abby balanced her coffee and phone while crunching through the old girl's gearbox. The irritating ping from her phone was courtesy of Matt.

Matt: *Victoria's expecting you at nine. Please tell me you're nearly there, or at least on your way?*

Abby balanced the coffee filled travel mug on her lap and stuck the phone to the magnetic holder covering the vent. Holding down the little blue mic on WhatsApp, she recorded a voice note.

"Yes, I've left." It was true, she had left, but there was no need to mention she hadn't reached the end of her street yet. "I'll be there for nine. Go back to your bed. You're ill remem—augh!" The speed bump, which Betty had just struck at a solid 38 mph, sent a slosh of coffee over her white shirt. The warm trickle that was seeping down her jeans and pooling in her crotch, didn't make the experience any better. It was at times like these Abby was grateful she drank nothing hot, instead opting for the cooler side of luke-warm. "It's fine. I'm fine. I'll be there."

And she was, with exactly ninety-seconds to spare. A miracle given the buildings in front of her weren't on any map. They were too new. Thank god Matt had told her the driveway she needed to find was on the first ninety degree bend, or else she'd have missed it completely. There were a series of renovated farm buildings at the end of the long mono blocked driveway, and Abby let out a long, low whistle as she took in the sheer scale of the project.

This must have cost them a small fortune. A quick glance around Betty's interior, with frayed stitching and stained velour seat covers made Abby cringe, especially when applied the groaning hand brake between a Mercedes SUV and Audi R8.

Maybe it was time to upgrade? That second hand Honda Civic she'd seen online, with under fifty thousand on the clock, was almost in her budget, and it wasn't bad for a five-year-old car—but now wasn't the time to think about that. First, she needed to change.

Creaking Betty's door open, Abby quickly glanced around. The place was quiet. Maybe too quiet? Had she got the right address? There had been no signs confirming the name of the property. It was just Matt's WhatsApp directions that had led to this spot. It would be wise to check the google coordinates... But before her thumb had swiped her iPhone screen, the right side of the large double oak door swung open to reveal a tall red headed woman and Abby's jaw hit the ground with a thud.

No. No way.

CHAPTER TWO

The slim redhead was moving towards her in easy strides, and she was talking. Abby was in too much shock to register any of the words, but she knew this woman was directing them all towards her. Before she could make any more sense of what was happening, she blurted out the only thing that was going through her head.

"Ms. Fraser?"

The red head stopped, drawing her head back just a little, and her smile changed to a curious yet playful frown as she considered Abby.

"Do I know you?"

How long had it been, thought Abby. Twelve years? No wait, if Abby was thirty-two, then it had to be—seventeen years. Seventeen years since she had appreciated this woman in the flesh, and seeing her again, Ms. Fraser was exactly as Abby had remembered her. No. No, that wasn't true. The woman was even more striking that Abby had recalled. How was it possible to age so well?

With a sudden cringe, Abby crossed her arms over her stomach in a vain attempt to hide the coffee splatter. The self-conscious action only drew attention to the exact thing she was trying to conceal.

"I'm Abby Mason," she offered nervously. The air of expectation that came with Abby's words seemed to land with confusion for the red-headed woman.

"Yes. Matt told me your name." Her reply was slow, as if she was talking to someone with comprehension difficulties.

Abby's face reddened. In all the daydreams she'd had about bumping into Ms. Fraser again, and there had been many, none of them had ever played out like this.

Still, the fizz of excitement in her stomach, as well as a little lower, was just as powerful now as it had been when it coursed through her hormone addled body as a teenager—if not more so. And the alarming wetness that was gathering between Abby's legs had nothing to do with the earlier Arabica blend which had seeped through the denim.

No, this was something quite different.

Abby fought to tear her eyes away from Ms. Fraser's lips, which were full and soft. But then she remembered the woman's fingers and her gaze dropped. Those long, elegant fingers that ran up and down the length of the thin baton as she leant over the polished wood of the Feurich Baby.

Abby's sister had played that piano so earnestly, almost as earnestly as Abby herself had studied Ms. Fraser. This woman had been her first sexual awakening, her deepest erotic fantasy, and her greatest investment of time.

Abby had spent an impossible number of hours imagining those grey-green eyes settling on her face, before travelling down her body. And wherever Ms. Fraser's eyes went, those long slender digits followed, exploring every inch of her fevered teenage skin—in her reveries. But sadly for Abby, never in reality.

And now she was standing in front of her. Abby swallowed hard and summoned all her courage.

"I'm Freya Mason's big sister. You used to come to our house to give her piano lessons." Abby's voice raised in question, seeking the older woman's acknowledgement. Ms Fraser blinked but didn't respond, so Abby blundered on. "My grandparents had the white cottage opposite the old Kirk at Cramond, and you'd come every Tuesday and Thursday afternoon. From four thirty 'til six." She paused, waiting for the information to slot into place.

The nod was slow but deliberate, and then a warm smile spread across the redhead's face and Abby's heart.

"Little Abby Mason." Ms. Fraser's head tilted as if she was letting memories pour from some old filing cabinet drawer. "You'd sit and read while your sister played. I don't think you ever missed a lesson." She chuckled. "How is Freya? I bumped into your grandmother a few years after I stopped teaching and she said she was at the Royal Conservatoire?"

Abby nodded. Freya had done well. She'd gotten her degree and masters while studying in Glasgow, and now she taught at the Guildhall in London.

Ms. Fraser seemed impressed when Abby reeled off her sister's achievements. Well, the ones I could remember, anyway. She shivered. The chill of the late spring morning still hung in the air, although Abby couldn't be sure if it was the weather that caused her body's response or the excitement of coming face to face with her teenage fantasy.

"You're cold. Let me help you grab your equipment and we can go inside. I've everything laid out in the studio ready for you." Victoria Fraser stepped forward, stretching out her hand, as if ready to carry whatever Abby might pass to her.

But the only thing Abby had readily available, was awkward hesitation.

"Is there somewhere I could...change?" Abby grimaced and stretched out her arms to reveal the full extent of the accident. "I spilt my coffee on the journey over."

The full abstract stain of her liquid breakfast seemed even darker in the daylight. It was a rich brown Rorschach inkblot. For two amused seconds, Abby thought about asking what the sexy Ms. Fraser saw, a bat or a butterfly, or perhaps an intimate moment between two—

Shit. Given today's shoot was for a lesbian website, did that mean Ms. Fraser was into women?

In every lust filled dream Abby had entertained about this woman, there had never been any doubt about Ms. Fraser's sexuality. She had unequivocally been into women, of course she had, it was after all Abby's fantasy. But that was all it was. Fantasy.

Wasn't it?

Holy heck, her teenage self would have died on the spot if she'd ever thought the red-headed siren might feel the same way about women as she did.

If Abby had been on her own, she'd have fist pumped. But she wasn't, so she didn't. But still...

"The studio has a large shower room. You can change there." Shaking her head, she added, "And call me Victoria. Ms. Fraser makes me feel so—old."

Abby was certain Victoria must have a picture in the attic, because she didn't look a day older than she remembered. *What age was she?*

Freya had attended St Mary's, a specialist education facility for the musically gifted, and Ms Fraser was completing her teacher training at the school, so that would have made her—twenty-three? Twenty-four maybe? A whole ten years older than the hormone ridden teenager Abby had been at the time.

The woman was only forty-two. That impossible gulf of an age gap that caused her teenage self so much angst was suddenly much smaller now and the woman obviously kept herself in good shape. The ivory sleeveless top Victoria wore over tailored black pants left her toned biceps in clear view. Abby stared at them as she handed over her large softbox frame and stand.

Today was just turning out *just fine*, as her grandmother would have said.

CHAPTER THREE

"The light in here is incredible." Abby had dumped her kit at the side and turned around, her arms wide, taking in the high vaulted space of what at one time would have been a huge milking barn. The stripped oak beams and selective areas of exposed brickwork were impressive, but they were nothing compared to what was in front of Abby as she came to a stop.

The entire south-facing wall of the building comprised of glass. The tri-folding doors sat beneath two huge triangular windows, allowing the soft Scottish light to flood into the space. It would be a nightmare to shoot here in the height of summer, but today was overcast. The soft, billowing clouds diffused the light with such a forgiving touch that Abby wished she was here to take Victoria's portrait, rather than a catalogue of product shots. It was criminal to block out such natural diffusion in favour of the pinpoint precision of speedlights and soft box. But she was here to shoot for the next two days and consistency counted, something the Scottish weather would never deliver.

Still, she took a few moments to indulge. Undulating

fields led the eye down to the silver shimmer of the River Forth. Steel grey clouds lined the far bank and the sun must have been breaking through somewhere, because the arch of a faint rainbow framed the view.

"It's quite something, isn't it?" The whispered heat of Victoria's breath tickled Abby's neck. Such was her rush to get out of the house this morning, she'd thrown her mousey brown waves up into a high ponytail. She stood quite still, savouring how close Victoria Fraser's body was to her own.

Closing her eyes for the briefest moment, she imagined Victoria's arms reaching around from behind and pulling her close. A ridiculous thought perhaps, but Abby had been so intimate with this woman, so many times in her imagination, that it was almost as natural as the light that washed over them.

"You can get changed through there."

Abby turned as Victoria stepped back and nodded towards a wooden door on the left. The moment had gone. With a final glance back over rolling fields, Abby realised that so had the rainbow.

Grabbing her backpack, she retreated to the large shower room, which was in fact a wet room. A dry wet room, but a wet room all the same. Using the loo, Abby took in her surroundings. It looked expensive. Victoria, or at least she presumed it had been Victoria, had covered the walls and floor in the same veined marble. There was a slight slope towards the shiny stainless-steel drain in the corner and oddly placed metal fixings on the wall.

She mused over the metal hooks, unable to fathom out how they would be utilised and then shrugged. Every new building had a raft of accessibility criteria they had to meet these days, so future proofing a room for new legislation was sensible, she supposed.

Having stripped off her coffee soiled clothes and now sporting her spare black T and ripped jeans, Abby took a moment to gather herself. This was weird and surreal. The thought of maybe bumping into Ms. Fraser at a club, exchanging numbers and having an illicit affair had crossed her mind many times and in great detail before she had met Katie. But then she fell in love. In real love, with a real person. Who left her in real pain when it had ended. She let out a long sigh.

"Right, get your professional head on, Abby," she told herself in a stern tone.

Pushing open the door, she walked across the room to where Victoria was leaning against the wall, watching her.

"Little Abby Mason. You're a blast from the past. It feels like a lifetime ago." Victoria shook her head, obviously as incredulous at the turn of events as Abby, albeit for very different reasons. "We're just through here."

Abby followed her through to a smaller room which contained a sofa and several theatre style seats on a long rack with wheels. A large oil painting of a naked woman tied to a four-poster bed took pride of place on one wall, but the focal point of the room was a window at the far end. Whatever was on the other side of the window was a mystery to Abby, because all she could see was darkness.

"This is the new range we need you to shoot." Victoria was walking towards a large table laden with stuff, and then hesitated. Turning back to face Abby she narrowed her eyes and asked, "Matt told you what the new range was, didn't he?"

Abby peered at the table. A pile of brown nondescript boxes took up space on one side, but a more intriguing array of leather, metal and fluff had been unpackaged next to them.

"Come closer, there's nothing here that'll bite...unless you want it to." Victoria smiled and beckoned Abby over. "It's all fairly light-hearted. Nothing too serious."

Abby stared at her workload. The thin black leather riding crops were the first thing that caught her attention. There were no two ways about it; she was seeing Ms. Fraser in a whole new light. PVC harnesses sat alongside handcuffs. Abby lifted them, allowing her fingers to rub the material. The softness surprised her, and she played with them as she scanned the rest of the items.

"You like being restrained?" Victoria's question caught her off guard, and she looked down towards her hands as her fingers continued to explore, feeling their way around the interior velvet of the cuffs.

"What? I—I've never used anything like this before. I was just curious. They're really soft." Abby placed the cuffs back onto the table and reached for the riding crop, aware of Victoria's gaze. "How do you go from being a music teacher to—this?"

Victoria laughed. "I suppose it must seem a bit of a leap, given your last memories of me. I'm both surprised and flattered you remembered who I was."

"I never forgot you," Abby's admission was out before she could stop herself and if Victoria Fraser didn't get the initial inference, the blush that rose the length of Abby's neck before vibrating from her cheeks made it explicit. "I mean, I..." her voice trailed off as she turned her attention back to the table.

"I always suspected you had a bit of a crush on me, but you were so young. Just a child—then."

"I was fourteen." Abby's tone sounded almost petulant.

"I remember your horrified look when your grandmother teased you. She thought you'd be able to play Freya's repertoire because you watched us so intently. Your face went as red then, as it is now." Placing a hand on Abby's arm, Victoria squeezed. "I'm sorry, I shouldn't tease. In answer to your question, a teacher's pay would never have given me the lifestyle I wanted, well, unless I married a rich husband. As you might have already guessed, that wasn't an option. Plus, I could never be open about my sexuality in a teaching position. Too many compromises and too little reward. Besides, I met Alison, and she opened up a whole new world to me."

"Is Alison your wife?" Abby wasn't sure she wanted to know the answer. The idea of Ms. Fraser being dropped back into her life, as a fully fledged lesbian, was the stuff of dreams. To give her a wife would just be cruel. Abby lifted what looked like two silver bull dog clips, held together on a short chain. "It's a bit different from a piano recital." Her fingers had to press so hard against the metal to open the clips, the colour drained from her nail bed. *Jesus. These things could rip your nipples clean off.*

Victoria reached across and slid her hand over Abby's, taking the clamps from her grasp. "Alison is not my wife. She was my partner, but that was many years ago. We made better business partners than life partners and *this...*" she said, holding up the clamps, "Is a lifestyle we both enjoy. I doubt there's anything left Alison hasn't tried. Let's just say she wanted to go to places that I'd never be comfortable with."

Abby's eyebrows raised, as her mouth formed a perfect O. There was a lot she didn't know about the whole BDSM scene, given her aversion to pain, but she did know there was usually a submissive partner while the other would be more dominant. Her eyes searched Victoria's face, willing herself to find the courage to ask, but she couldn't be that bold. Under Victoria's intent gaze, she looked away.

The touch of those smooth, long fingers that Abby had yearned for as a teenager slid under her chin, titling it upwards until their eyes met. Abby swallowed hard, trying to contain the surge of excitement that shot through her body.

"You know the answer." Victoria didn't blink and Abby didn't dare move. There was so much more to Victoria Fraser than Abby had reckoned. The woman was spell-binding.

"Right. Shall we get this show on the road?" Victoria turned, leaving Abby grasping for the edge of the table, wondering what the hell had just happened.

CHAPTER FOUR

The shoot went off without a hitch. Once you'd got your set up sorted for each of the grouped products, based on how reflective the material was, the required background and so forth, product shoots were a breeze. It was one of the many wonders of an environment over which you had complete control. And the exact reason Abby avoided them. Where was the thrill when you couldn't give yourself over to a little chaos?

The products themselves made this shoot more interesting and as Victoria had held up each restraint, clamp or cuff, for Abby to place and shoot, she couldn't help but acknowledge a growing tingle of arousal.

Working methodically, Abby unhooked her Nikon D850 from the stand, pressing the release and removing the VR lens, to pack it away for the night. Most of her equipment would stay in situ ready for tomorrow, but she never left her camera.

It was a little after seven and Abby stretched out her tired limbs. Victoria's voice was a muffled echo from the next room, the sound reverberating around the vaulted space. Being left to her own devices, curiosity led her to the huge, darkened window. The bottom was about a foot from the floor and it stretched almost the full height of the room, stopping about a foot from the ceiling. It was one hell of a slab of glass, that was for sure, but for what purpose?

In an earlier conversation, Abby had subtly enquired about what was on the other side of the glass, but Victoria had ignored it, focussing on the job at hand. But now, with Victoria's attention elsewhere, Abby approached it and peered through. There were faint outlines, but with everything shrouded in darkness, it was difficult to define what the shapes might be. Cupping her hands around the edge of her vision to block out the light, Abby pressed her face against the window. There was something wide and low in the centre of the space, something that was raised on a platform.

What the hell was it?

Scanning the wall, she found a couple of switches and flicking them plunged the room into complete black. If she could make it back to the window without breaking her neck on a cable, chair or similar, then she'd be able to see what was on the other side.

"Ouch," her involuntary cry came as her hip collided with the corner of the table. There was little to no padding to shield her, given her impromptu weight loss brought on after Katie's departure. With a grimace, she swallowed the pain, wondering if this was just a ridiculous idea. It was probably a bloody store cupboard. But why would you have a window looking into a store cupboard? Her hand pressed against her hip, which would probably be black and blue by tomorrow. Victoria was still on the phone, so she pressed on.

One whacked knee, and a little light cursing, and her face made contact with the glass. The outline she'd seen before was a bed. She was looking at the biggest super king bed she had ever seen. It was bigger than the massive mattress that filled the tent at the Golden Triangle jungle place in Thailand where she and Katie had honeymooned. Back then they'd joked about the fact they could have fitted another ten people into bed with them, but the one on the other side of the glass was even bigger. She was still contemplating the who, what, and why of the situation when something rubbed against her body.

Eyes wide, she stiffened. There was definitely something or someone there. And someone with far better night vision than her own, obviously.

"Are you okay?"

Abby squealed like a child as fright oozed out of every pore. How the hell had Victoria got behind her with such stealth and without tripping over anything? How the hell had she opened the door without light pouring into the room and then she remembered the blackout curtain that covered the entrance.

One loud clap and the lights clicked on. Abby blinked in an attempt to adjust to the sudden brightness. A highly amused Victoria stood smiling, with her head cocked to one side.

"The lights are sound controlled. Did you switch them off by accident or—?"

Victoria's unanswered question hung in the air, offering Abby a choice. Take the out offered or be candid about why she was peering through an oddly placed window. She opted for candid.

"I wanted to see what was on the other side of the glass." She gave a lame shrug. "I've been staring at it all day." Abby nodded towards the glass. "I wanted to see what was on the other side and I couldn't see with the light on, so...I banged my hip and my—"

"You've cut your knee." Victoria leant forward and wiped a smear of blood through the rip in Abby's jeans. "I've plasters in the house." She pointed toward where Abby had parked at the start of the day and then broke into a grin. "If you'd asked, I'd have shown you around." Then, softening her tone, Victoria moved a little closer. "There's really no need to sneak around in the dark. I'm happy to satisfy your curiosity, besides you've another day of shooting tomorrow and I need you in one piece."

Abby gave a shy nod. Blindly stealing around in the dark had been ridiculous and where there had been curiosity, there was now only mortification. Victoria must have sensed the younger woman's discomfort because she lightly grasped the top of Abby's arms and faced her straight on. There was about three inches of height difference between them and Abby had to look up as Victoria spoke.

"Why don't we order some food. You can stay over. There are eight bedrooms, seven of which are yet to be occupied by anyone, so you'd be helping me finish the snagging list that Alison keeps nagging me to do. Then we can head across to the studio first thing in the morning and I'll give you the full guided tour."

Victoria's expression was warm, open and most of all kind. The one thing that had been lacking in Abby's life since Katie had left, or maybe even longer, but she just hadn't had the courage to acknowledge it at the time.

The thought of driving back to Edinburgh and searching for a place to park didn't fill her with excitement. Her basement apartment on Forth Street had plenty of designated residents' parking, but given the proximity to the city centre, it was nigh on impossible to find a parking space after eight in the evening.

Fresh sheets, a warm house, and hot food sounded perfect. Plus, it would be good to have company. It would help her unwind.

"What do you say?" Victoria touched a loose curl that fallen from Abby's messy ponytail and tucked it behind her ear. It was a simple gesture, but the rush of Victoria's touch against her cheek caused Abby's breath to hitch and, without thinking, she pressed her cheek against those long elegant fingers. Exhilaration shot through her torso, culminating in an unmistakable twitch between her legs, before rebounding back to complete the circuit. But there was something else...as if that wasn't enough, and Abby struggled to name the sensation. Safety? Trust? Familiarity? Maybe it was one of those or a combination of all of them. She didn't know. But it felt—good. Really good.

Losing herself in the emerald flecks of Victoria's eyes, Abby felt a hand slide down her arm and take her hand. Her fingers, calloused from lugging around camera equipment, wrapped around the older woman's smooth, warm skin and, in a moment of bravery, she squeezed. The feather light stroke of a thumb over her palm sent a rolling wave of desire through her body making her knees weak. Of course, that may also have been down to a lack of food, but there was one thing she knew for sure; tomorrow she was going to have to go commando.

CHAPTER FIVE

"So what was it Alison wanted that you couldn't give her?" Abby nestled in the corner of the sofa, with her glass of soda. Victoria had been curious about Abby's choice of beverage. The younger woman had assured her that opting for the soft drink was down to her desire to keep a clear head for tomorrow.

"We've still got work to do," she'd said with a smile, but was it *that* desire that had driven the request for something non-alcoholic? After the way Abby had brushed her cheek against Victoria's hand earlier in the evening, she suspected there was more to it.

The awkward teenager who had spent hours mesmerised by her every move had vanished and in her place was a beautiful, talented and funny woman.

Abby's teenage crush had been obvious and at the time it had been only an amusing aside for her, although she was very sure that the intense young Abby had found no humour, only unrequited yearning. She was so lost in the memory of Abby, Freya, their grandmother and the white homely cottage they'd lived in, she hadn't answered Abby's question. And Abby obviously wanted an answer because she asked again.

"You said earlier that Alison wanted more than you could give her?" The lift at the end of Abby's sentence made it clear she was looking for a response. As clear as the fact, she wasn't letting it go. The obvious curiosity about their lifestyle, which Abby kept circling, reminded Victoria of mating Herring Gulls. She used to watch them when she'd walked along the coast in late spring. The females would rotate around the male, demanding attention. The volume of the squawks got louder until it was impossible for them to be ignored.

Victoria found Abby's want for her attention flattering, now more so than when they'd first met. For one, the attraction was no longer one sided. The mousey brown hair that Abby had roughly shoved up into a loose ponytail while she'd been working was now down, gently caressing her shoulders, and following the deep V of her black T-shirt. The swell of what Victoria imagined to be perfectly formed breasts teased out from behind the dark cotton. Abby was perfect in so many ways—a natural sub.

Victoria bit her lip, trying desperately not to let what she was thinking, or more accurately feeling, on the inside, show on the outside. There was a ten-year age gap, for god's sake. Did that make her some sort of cougar? Wait, could you even be a cougar if your desire was for women, not men?

For a brief second, she considered googling the lesbian equivalent—what would it be? A jaguar? A lynx? A bobcat? That really would be her luck.

"Victoria?" The sound of Abby saying her name pulled her back into the room. "I'm not making you relive painful memories am I? You seemed deep in thought?"

If only you knew what I was thinking, my sweet little Abby, she mused.

"Alison enjoys elements I don't." She watched Abby's eyebrows knit together when she said the word *elements*. "My hard limits are just that, hard limits. I'm clear about what I enjoy and I stay within my boundaries. Alison is all about pushing boundaries. In the end, the journey she wanted to take as a submissive meant that I was the wrong mistress for her. There was no great drama. It was all very amicable." Her hand gave a dismissive gesture, as if the pain of the breakup she had felt so acutely had been a mere tickle.

The truth was, the split had left her in a state of devastation. The knowledge that you are not enough for the woman you love had filled hours of airtime for Victoria and her therapist. But from the stories that Abby had shared about her own divorce earlier in the evening, Victoria knew she'd understand.

"What elements?" Abby asked in an almost whisper.

People were always curious about their lifestyle choices and often asked questions. Not so much of Victoria, but most definitely of Alison and Mhairi. Mhairi—the woman—the mistress, who had fulfilled all of Alison's desires. While Victoria was, as Alison teased, a *lightweight*. Nobody could ever say that of Mhairi.

There had been a tremble in Abby's voice. Was it down to insecurity about having the right to ask, or was she afraid of the answer? Victoria had a talent for reading people, but she wasn't sure. Abby deserved more respect than having her jump to an assumption or an incorrect conclusion. That was Victoria's thought process, but what came out of her mouth didn't quite match.

"What people desire is nobody's business but their

own." She cringed when she heard the harshness of the words burst from her mouth. She was a woman that helped develop people's self-esteem, for god's sake, not strip it down.

Abby's head lowered and her body tightened as a quiet, "I'm sorry," escaped her lips. The younger woman had been so open about her divorce, and the death of her grandparents, who, except for Freya, had been her only family. Every question Victoria had asked, and there were many, had been answered with warmth and vulnerability. And then what did Victoria do?

She made Abby feel bad about asking her a simple question.

This woman, for whom she was rapidly developing a fondness, was just curious. She didn't deserve the abruptness of Victoria's reply.

"I'm sorry, that was harsh. It's true but—," Placing her water glass on the table, she moved to sit next to Abby. Perched on the edge of the sofa, with her body turned to face her, she offered a softer response. "Perhaps if we change the question? What If I tell you what my hard limits are? And for complete transparency, the breadth of my hard limits was wider than Alison's desires. I'm a tourist by her standards."

Victoria offered an apologetic smile and waited. The ball was in Abby's court. The young woman needed to be listened to, as well as feeling in control of what came next. "Does that sound like a plan?"

"I'd like that." Her accompanying grin was sheepish, but sincere.

"Good." Victoria patted her leg and then explained. "I'm a mistress who likes to empower their submissive."

Abby's face contorted in confusion, causing Victoria to laugh.

"I know that sounds weird and confusing. Let me explain. The irony is that the sub in any healthy relationship, and by healthy, I mean a relationship of equals, based on trust and respect, holds as much, if not more, power than the dominant partner. It's about connection and a consensual power exchange. And one word can stop it from either person. I'm assuming you've heard of safe words and hard limits?"

Abby nodded and opened her mouth as if to speak, but stopped herself.

"Don't be frightened to say whatever is on your mind. Honesty and communication are healthy."

"I've read stuff, mainly fictional stuff," Abby said dismissively and then a thought seemed to hit her. "Lesbian fiction, not heteronormative stuff," she clarified.

Victoria smiled. Abby was such a millennial.

"But I always thought that the safe word and boundaries were for the sub? Is that a stupid question?" Abby screwed up her face, unable to hide how vulnerable she was obviously feeling. *Lord, this woman is glorious.* Victoria caught herself before she once again slipped down the lust filled rabbit hole of imagining a naked Abby, restrained and oh, so eager to please.

"It isn't a stupid question, and it's a common misconception. Both of you need to feel comfortable and turned on. It's about pleasure, not pressure. I love restraining my partner, driving them wild with sensation, or denying them. It's a turn on, but my list of boundaries, or limits, is fairly extensive." She chuckled. "I'm far too vanilla for a lot of subs. I'm uncomfortable applying pain that goes beyond spanking or whipping.

Likewise, I'd never be a match for a sub that gets turned on by humiliation or knife play…" Victoria paused, aware of how wide Abby's eyes had grown. She was hiding behind her glass of soda.

"Sorry, you don't want to hear all this. I get how alarming it must sound if it's not your thing." Just as she turned to move out of Abby's space, a hand around her wrist stopped her.

"But what if it was?" Abby said. "Not the pain thing, but being tied up? Told what to do?" The young woman's eyes were dark, and nervously bit her lip. "Does that mean I'm a submissive?"

Seriously, thought Victoria, *how did I not see this coming?*

She wrapped her hand around Abby's fingers, which were still clinging tightly. "It's late. We should both get some sleep. Wanting somebody to take the lead in the bedroom doesn't mean you're a sub. Even the most vanilla of couples have days where they want somebody to take charge. Being a sub is more complex than that. I don't think you have anything to worry about."

Victoria held out her hand and stood. "Come with me and I'll show you where you're sleeping."

CHAPTER SIX

"She stayed with you the whole day?" Matt was incredulous. "Shit. I'm lucky if I see them for ten minutes. I get my instructions, be told to be a good boy, and then they disappear." He let out a pondering humph of air through his nose, which only caused him to cough. He sounded terrible. "I wonder why she hung around?"

Abby didn't know the answer to the question, but was glad she had. Victoria was fun, interesting and incredibly engaging—and not just mentally. She squirmed in the bed, thinking about how the touch of red heads fingers had felt against her cheek. Her whole body had lit up with pleasure.

"Who knows? It's the first time I've done a job for them, so maybe she wanted to make sure I got what they were after?"

"Mm. Maybe." Matt didn't sound convinced. "The new place is wild though, isn't it. Imagine booking that place as your Airbnb. You'd get way more than you imagined." The laugh that followed sent him into a spluttering mess.

Airbnb? She hadn't seen that coming.

"I'm getting the full tour tomorrow. I spent most of the

day in one room. The shots are clean, though, and it won't take long to edit when I get back tomorrow." Abby touched her cheek, pushing away a curl of mousey brown hair before tucking it behind her ear. Would Victoria spend the day with her again or would she just disappear as she'd done with Matt? She knew what she'd like to happen, but...

"What time did you finish? I got stuck on that bloody bridge for almost an hour last time. Some arse had gone into the back of a Porsche. There was bugger all damage, but it brought everyone fleeing Fife to a standstill."

"Oh, I'm still here. Victoria offered, and it made sense to stay. I'll get an earlier start in the morning and I might get finished early too, if I'm lucky."

The line went silent. No coughs, groans or even the vaguest hint of a wheeze.

Abby took the phone from her ear and tapped the screen. A blue hazy light replaced the darkness. The rising seconds on the call time meant they were still connected.

"Matt?"

After a couple of seconds, she heard a heavy breath followed by a sniff. "You're staying the night?" He sounded almost amused.

"I'm in one of the guest rooms. Just me, on-my-own. Get your mind out of the gutter." Taking the moral high-ground was a tad ironic given the thoughts she'd been having all day, but she wasn't ready to share. Not yet. "Listen, it's late and I need to get some sleep. I'll call you when I get back tomorrow. Okay?"

There were so many questions that Abby had about this place, the studio, as well as Victoria and she could have asked him, but she chose not to. Let it all unfold naturally, she thought to herself with a small smile.

They agreed to talk again once Abby was home and

they ended the call, but not before Matt teased her about how much Victoria must be *enjoying* her company. He was probably worried she'd nick his client.

Abby hooked her phone to the charger then starfished across the bed. Even with every limb fully stretched towards the four corners, she was still miles from the edge. The smoothness of the thick cotton sheets beneath her body caused her to sigh in appreciation. They probably cost more than she was being paid for the two-day shoot. The sleepwear that Victoria had handed her was still in a neatly folded pile on the velvet padded bench which ran along the foot of the bed. Wearing clothes to bed had always felt alien to her. Even in the depths of winter, she slept naked. There was no way she was going to deny her skin the luxury of what must be a million thread count, it felt too good.

A thousand thoughts cascaded through her head and nine hundred and ninety-nine of them involved Victoria. The only non-erotic musing was a vague concern about tomorrow's lack of fresh underwear, but that could wait. Instead, she allowed her imagination to roam. Eyes fluttering closed, she pictured soft rope she'd photographed earlier, wrapped around her wrists. Moving her shoulders, she could almost feel the knots tighten. Then, turning her attention to her ankles, she imagined the same material anchor the lower half of her body. Spread eagled, unable to move, she surrendered to the dark figure coming towards her. A hitched breath escaped and echoed around the room. A small squirm and the wetness between her legs pooled. What would Ms. Fraser do to her? A whimper escaped her lips, followed by a single word, "Please." God, she wanted this so much. To relinquish all control and surrender.

To Victoria.

The weight of the comforter covering her naked skin

became the weight of her—her Mistress. Oh, to have Victoria as her mistress. An image of the woman leaning against a piano, running a baton through her hand, so gently, caused Abby to moan and squirm. The sateen material gilding over her skin were now fingers. Her mistress's fingers, claiming Abby for her own. Every tiny movement of the material sent waves of desire coursing through her. She let out a long, low groan, giving into the sensations flooding over her.

"Victoria, please," Abby's voice trembled in the darkness of the room.

She was going to come...without a single touch, she was going to climax. Fuck.

A floorboard creaked but she couldn't stop the small strangled cry erupting from her chest. She was too far gone.

"Come for me."

The thunder of white noise crashed through her ears, annihilating everything except the all-consuming explosion of pleasure. Wave after wave of sensation cracked through her body until it left her in a heap of tremors, gasping for breath.

Eventually, when her breathing had calmed enough for her to move, she wrapped her arms around her body, and curled into a ball, holding herself tight.

Had somebody spoken to her? "Come for me." Those were the words she thought she'd heard. Had it been real? It had sounded like... Victoria. Had she imagined it? Maybe she had. After all, she'd never been able to come without touching herself, until now, so if she could do that, couldn't she just as easily have imagined hearing the words? The words she so desperately wanted Victoria to say to her.

Bracing herself on shaky arms, she sat up and looked around the darkened room. After a few seconds, her eyes adjusted and the outline of the chair where she'd abandoned her clothes earlier came into view. Had she expected to see Victoria sitting there? Or was her desire so strong that hope was clouding her judgement? Whatever it might be, there was a sense of disappointment in finding nothing but her sad looking workwear.

With a thump, her sweaty body slumped back down onto the mattress, alone.

CHAPTER SEVEN

The smell of coffee rose the wide sweeping staircase before seeping into the bedroom. Abby roused and blinked. It took a moment to find her bearings. This wasn't her bed. No, she was in Victoria's house...or Airbnb, or whatever it was. That was one of the many questions she might get answers to today, or at least hoped she would. But it wasn't time to get up, was it? With an enormous yawn, she stretched out, arms and legs pointing to every corner of the huge mattress. There was just enough time to indulge in one last starfish before she had to get up. She spread herself just as she had done before she fell asleep...when she had—

Her eyes went wide and in frantic movements she ran her hands over the thick smooth cotton sheet. Feeling nothing but warm, expensive bedding, her body flopped back down. There was no evidence of the previous night's excitement. *Thank Christ for that.*

There was a light knock on the door.

"Come in." Abby's warm, rich tone surprised even her. Perhaps last night had loosened things up a little.

The door eased open, and Victoria appeared, smiling

warmly in an outfit decidedly more casual than the business attire she wore yesterday.

"I thought you might like some fresh clothes and clean underwear?"

Abby went to speak and stopped herself. Underwear? She hesitated, unsure of how she felt about something so intimate...to wear Victoria's underwear? But then again, after last night.

Jesus, that was a just a dream, Abby, get a grip.

Victoria seemed to know what she was thinking. "The sweats and tank are mine. They'll be too long for you, but once you've got your sneakers on, I don't think it'll matter. The underwear is a sample from an Italian company. They want us to be the online retailers for the UK." She paused. "Anyway, they are new and I think they're your size."

"Thanks." Without thinking, Abby pushed herself up from the bed as if she was about to make her way to where Victoria stood. In a flash she realised her mistake. With the top half of her naked body in full view, she stopped, flushed a violent shade of red, but didn't move. Neither did Victoria.

Their eyes held the others for what seemed like a very long minute until Victoria blinked. But instead of looking away as Abby expected, the older woman allowed her gaze to drop, taking in every inch of exposed flesh. The way Victoria bit down on her lip was enough to let Abby know the view was being appreciated, and *that* caused an involuntary twitch of excitement to ripple between her legs. She didn't dare move. If telepathy was a real thing, then Victoria would have known that Abby wanted nothing more than to hear an explicit instruction demanding her surrender. If only Victoria would just take her.

But that wasn't what happened.

As much as Abby might have wanted the situation to

escalate, and she hadn't mistaken the look desire on Victoria's face, it was impossible to miss, that wasn't how their morning started.

Instead, Victoria strode into the room, placed the fresh clothes at the end of the bed and picked up the unused sleepwear before walking back towards the door. "Breakfast is ready, shower and be down in ten."

Victoria left the bedroom door wide open, and a naked Abby remained on the bed, lips parted.

————

Showered and wearing the new underwear from "Segreti," the company courting Victoria and Alison's favour, under grey sweatpants and tank, Abby wandered into the large kitchen. The silk of the panties felt great against her skin and her nipples responded to the slight roughness of the lace bra. They were red, not a tacky, garish red but a deep ruby colour, which even under sweats made Abby feel classy. The company had delicately embroidered three words on the front of the panties, "io sono tua." Abby knew it was Italian, but given she didn't speak the language, she didn't know what it meant. She'd google it later.

The room had a full glass wall that looked over the same fields that she'd seen in the studio yesterday. It would be beautiful in summer, when you could haul open the doors and let the day in. But just like the grounds surrounding the studio, there was still landscaping work to be completed. A large island dominated the centre of the kitchen, with several stools tucked neatly underneath. Placing a large cup of steaming coffee on the island, Victoria indicated for Abby to sit.

Pulling out the wide based stool, she hauled her ass up

and settled on its grey leather padded seat. It was surprisingly comfortable. Victoria placed a platter of fresh fruit along with two forks in the centre of the table. She had two smaller plates ready for them and she offered one to Abby. Everything in the kitchen had its own space and was exactly placed. It couldn't be farther removed from Abby's own galley kitchen. The previous owners had shoehorned it into what had once been a closet. To sit down and eat breakfast in her place, she'd have to move the microwave and sit on the washing machine. As Matt would say...any excuse.

"Given the stain on your shirt yesterday, I guessed coffee; black. Do you need sugar?"

Abby shook her head.

"I've some oats in the cupboard, if you prefer? I've a strict, no gluten diet so I can't offer you toast or..." her voice trailed off as if she was working what other carb ridden goodies she'd struck from her diet.

"The fruit's good. Thanks." Abby stuck her fork into a cube of melon and lifted it towards her mouth. "I usually just grab a coffee in the morning." Her shrug was apologetic, like she was sharing some weird guilty secret and saying it out loud brought relief. She imagined herself in a circle of people, standing up, and saying, "My name is Abby, and I drink breakfast...and not in a healthy, smoothy sort of way."

Victoria eyed her with intent. Although what that intent might be, Abby had no idea. But right now, in this kitchen, on this island, which was just about the right height... Fuck.

"I've been thinking," Victoria said, slicing straight through Abby's melon sucking daydream. "The photographer Alison had arranged for promoting this place has fallen through. He got a better offer from a Swedish property company, or something like that, and we haven't gotten around to finding a replacement. I'd like you to do it, if you're willing?"

Abby's face contorted. The slice of blood orange she so eagerly bit into was a cunningly disguised piece of grapefruit; her fruit nemesis. With one eye tight shut and the other wide, her eyebrow merged with her hairline and she sucked in her cheeks, an unwilling slave to the tartness.

Victoria laughed. A full bellied warm laugh that made Abby want to take another bite, just so she could hear it again. It was glorious. Without another thought, she said, "I'm willing."

Victoria's smiling eyes narrowed in approval. "Good girl. Then eat up, I'll give you a tour and explain what we're after."

Today was going to be a great day. Abby could just feel it...in all the right places.

CHAPTER EIGHT

As Abby chomped her way through more than half of the large platter of fruit, which was not bad for a "strictly no solids before midday" sort of girl, Victoria laid out her and Alison's latest venture. This was, as Matt had said, an Airbnb, of sorts, but it wouldn't be your average tourists that would be paying the four-figure nightly fee. They, Victoria and Alison, had designed the entire place for small groups of like-minded individuals who enjoyed a little kink.

The way Victoria was describing the odd partnership with her ex suggested to Abby that the design was more Alison's sphere while Victoria was the business brains behind it all. Back in the nineties, a trans woman friend had come to them with the idea of giant padded panties, something that could be worn under clothing to offer a more womanly figure. Alison, a sculpture major at the Edinburgh College of Art, the same college Abby had graduated from, designed their new product range; for all sizes and shapes, while Victoria crunched the numbers to make it viable. Crystal, their friend, looked after everything marketing and between them, they made a small fortune exporting all over the world to their niche market. From there, they created several more highly lucrative companies all centred around adult themes. The latest project, the house and studio were just ways of spending surplus profit before the tax man spent it for them.

Abby nodded, unable to even fathom how many zeros you'd have at the end of your bank statement for this to be a side project. The main house in which they sat was the accommodation block. Abby nearly laughed at Victoria's description. She'd made it sound like something out of Wentworth, but this was as far removed from an institution as Abby could imagine. Perhaps Lou Kelly would have been less likely to blow the place up if she'd had Egyptian cotton sateen sheets.

But the studio sounded like something Joan Ferguson would have designed. Abby's head swam with all the information she was being given. According to Victoria, the studio contained a variety of architectural pieces, including a double St Andrews cross, whatever that was, as well as benches, stocks and even a full size viewing room. At least that last bit made sense now. But having spent the whole of yesterday in amongst the catalogue of devices Victoria had listed, it left her with one question: How the heck had she missed it all?

No wonder Abby's announcement of staying the night had stunned Matt into silence. Did he know about all of this? He must have. But did that mean he was into... Abby's brain was exploding. The most outrageous thing Victoria had handed her yesterday was a spreader bar, but that seemed so vanilla after this morning's revelations.

"Is this too much?" Victoria leant across and touched Abby's hand.

"What? Oh, no." Then, remembering their previous

night's conversation about honesty and communication, she said, "It's a bit—*heavier,* than I expected. I sort of get turned on by the submissive thing." Her face flushed scarlet. "I can even imagine how the being watched would be..." her voice trailed off. "But some of it sounds painful."

Victoria laughed, much to Abby's delight because the mirth filling the room was not at what she'd said, but in an understanding of her trepidation.

"I get it. It can sometimes feel like being a vegan walking into Brazilian Steakhouse. If you're not eating, then you must be on the menu." Victoria laughed again as Abby's eyes widened.

Jesus, thought Abby, *I could spend all day just making this woman laugh.*

"But that's not what it's really like. I promise. There's a vast spectrum of choice and you just need to find your place in the colour chart. But safely. Have you finished?" Victoria nodded to the now small amount of fruit left on the table.

"Yes. Thanks."

"Then let's start your education."

CHAPTER NINE

Abby watched as Victoria slid back the painting on the wall. The large antique rug which had covered the centre of the room yesterday was nowhere to be seen. *Bloody hell,* thought Abby. *What time had Victoria gotten up this morning?*

As instructed Abby sat on the brightly coloured chaise lounge, her fingers running across its soft fabric. It was a vibrant red; it reminded her of her grandmother's jam, bubbling away on the stovetop. The life their grandparents had given both her and her sister had been secure and loving. Katie, her ex-wife, who was a social worker, had said they were trying to make up for the fact she and Freya had lost both parents within a year.

There was some truth to that. Losing her father first to a brain aneurysm was cruel, but when her mother joined him exactly one year later, thanks to a stockpile of prescription diazepam, all she could recall was a surreal numbness. She'd been nine years old.

But her grandparents had been good people. It wasn't compensation they'd offered, but pure unconditional love. It was just who they were. Abby missed that love. According to Katie, it's what made her needy (and why she loved Disney). Fuck Katie.

A glass panel illuminated the space where the painting had hung. Victoria placed her palm against it. A light scanned the surface. *Well, this is all a little Star Trek,* Abby thought. The screen changed, and a menu appeared. Victoria's finger lightly tapped and within seconds, a low rumble rose through the room. A queer, although not unpleasant, vibration tickled Abby's feet. And then the floor parted. Literally divided, sliding back and out. She half expected Moses to appear. Then, to her complete amazement, a huge wooden structure rose through the gaping wound.

Holy shit, this wasn't something you saw every day.

Abby sat open mouthed, and stared. With a clunk, the undercurrent of mechanical whirring that had filled the room faded out, leaving only silence. In front of her was a huge wooden sculpture. It was stunning—and massive. The soft illumination of fresnel lighting caused the wood to glint. While the impact was minimal in the light of the day, Abby could imagine the effect at night. The hard edges of teak had been removed and replaced with an elegant flow, making it look like driftwood. Abby had an urge to touch it.

"The St. Andrew's double cross. Alison's design." Victoria announced.

"It's like a piece of art." Tearing her eyes away to look at Victoria, she asked, "May I touch it?"

"Of course."

There was something—erotic, about the hard warmth of the wood. Each saltire cross took strength from the other, joining at the top, and then splayed towards the floor. Abby slipped between them, running her hands over their length.

The metal of the hooks, which her finger tips traced, were cold; a stark contrast to the body of the piece.

"Come this side." Victoria held out her hand and Abby took it. With a gentle grace, the younger woman allowed herself to be guided to the front of the cross. The firmness of Victoria's hands on her quads took her by surprise, as did the closeness of their bodies. Sliding palms between her thighs, Victoria eased Abby's legs apart until they rested against Alison's work. The option to play it cool and collected disappeared when she gasped. Abby wanted nothing more than to feel Victoria's hands run higher up her body.

And they did.

But rather than focus on Abby's growing excitement, which was making itself known on the new panties, Victoria's hands ran up Abby's body in one continuous movement. The tank rose to bare a glimpse of tattooed flesh, before thumbs momentarily rubbed lace against eager nipples, then pushed arms skyward against the hardness of the cross to which she was now pinned. Pinned by Victoria's body.

They were both wearing loose sweats, making everything so easily accessible. A small shift of Victoria's weight to the foot balanced between Abby's thighs, and that tiny added pressure in just the right place, was all it took. Abby let out a low guttural groan and a slow smile spread across Victoria's face. The redhead's green eyes sparkled. Then she stepped back, leaving Abby spread eagled and desperate, just as she had been the night before.

But this time rather than hearing the words "Come for me," as she'd imagined last night (or had she?) Victoria said, "Let me show you downstairs."

Fuck.

With a shudder, Abby wrapped her arms around her

body and followed. Every one of her senses was on high alert and she had to break into a trot to catch up. When Victoria stopped at the large bookcase on the back wall, she had no choice than to make an abrupt stop behind her.

Abby shot her a quizzical look.

"Open for me." On Victoria's command, the bookcase slid to the right, revealing a metal door with a touchpad, similar to the one which had appeared from behind the picture. Again, Victoria placed her palm on the dark glass and the door slid open. "We programme the biometrics when each group arrives. That way, they choose who controls access."

A series of spotlights lit the stairs down to the large space. It wasn't dark or vaguely dungeon like, with black painted walls as Abby had imagined. It was a bright space... with a cage in the corner.

Evidently aware of Abby's discomfort Victoria, placed a reassuring hand on her arm. "It's a spectrum," she said. "We can partition off areas either physically or with lighting." Then, lowering her voice, she gave two orders, "Zonal Lightning. Couch only."

The low, commanding voice made Abby shudder; in a good way.

For a second, the entire room fell into darkness. Then, with a theatrical flair befitting London's West End, a single soft light fell across an oddly shaped chaise lounge. It was as though this was the only thing in the room and the cage had disappeared. Victoria gestured towards the light with a sweeping hand and Abby walked towards it.

"The curves allow support for different positions. Restraints can be attached to the hooks." Abby squinted. In front of her was an exquisite piece of furniture. She would have never seen the hasps if Victoria hadn't pointed them out. Alison had obviously taken some inspiration from the classic Chesterfield, and Abby reckoned the dark leather would make it easy to clean. Victoria lifted a discarded short riding crop that lay on the cushion. The older woman ran it through her fingers as though she too remembered the music baton. Abby's insides shook.

"Bend across its curves and get a feel for it." This time, Victoria's words were softer, making it feel more of a suggestion than an order. Abby wondered if it was in response to her reaction to seeing the cage.

Running her hand along the curves, Abby took in the cool, stiff leather. The suppleness would come with use, but for now everything was new. She stopped at one end. The height was perfect, and she leant forward, parting her legs a little. "Like this?" she asked coyly.

Abby swallowed as she felt the warmth of Victoria's body behind her.

"Your legs need to be a little wider."

A foot kicked towards Abby's sneakers, forcing her legs farther apart.

Not feet, I want your hands. She was mentally willing Victoria to slide down the loose sweats and take her right there and then. But she didn't. Instead, Victoria stood very still. Abby could feel her warmth. That beautiful firm body was right next to her, and she'd spread herself wide open in offer, but frustratingly, nothing happened.

Abby wanted to scream.

"We've still got the exhibitionist's room to show you." Victoria said, but as she turned, her hand brushed high against the top of Abby's inner thigh. Abby's breath hitched, but before she could fathom whether the move had been accidental or deliberate, Victoria had stepped away. "Zonal lighting off."

The entire space was once again immersed in light. Straightening up, Abby squirmed to loosen the sodden silk which had attached itself to her centre. The cage was back in view, as were a set of stocks and some rather serious looking benches, all of which she hadn't seen before, primarily because she had been so horrified at seeing a cage. Rows of whips and floggers, in presentation cases, lined the walls next to an array of moveable shackles that appeared to be on tracks. Height adjustable. How practical.

There was an element of relief when they made their way back up to ground level. As much as having Victoria so close to her had been both frustrating and delicious, there was more in the basement that gave her discomfort than excitement. But would Victoria be less interested in her if she admitted that?

The bed seemed even bigger, as did the window, now she was on the other side of the glass which she had peered through yesterday. Crisp white sateen sheets were so tightly spread across the bed Abby reckoned she could have bounced a coin on the surface.

Given the place is so new, has anyone 'done' anything on the bed? She wondered.

"Try it out. I think this might be more your thing." Victoria offered a warm smile.

"It's so perfect. I'll just crease it."

"You're supposed to be helping me with snagging, remember?"

Bashfully, although in truth, there wasn't that much encouragement needed, Abby stepped up onto the platform and climbed on the bed. The pose she chose was the one which had been so much fun last night. Starfished to every corner, she again closed her eyes, imagining the restraints.

"So the idea of being tied up turns you on?" Victoria's

breath whispered against her ear, causing Abby to inhale fast and deep. The red head was on the platform just behind her. "Imagine a row of people sitting behind that glass watching you. They're all here to see me take you. To claim you." Victoria's hand reached over Abby's shoulder, running her fingertips along the smooth skin of her collar-bone and then down.

"Oh, god," Abby groaned.

"They're here to watch you come. Again and again. So many times..." Victoria's hand was sliding down over Abby's stomach.

"Please." Abby's plea had an edge of desperation that couldn't even begin to convey her need. This was beyond anything she had experienced, and the only thing that scared her was that it might stop.

There was a slight crackle, as though a static energy was filling the air, and then, without warning, every light came to life. Victoria's hand stilled.

"Alison and Mhairi are here." Victoria nodded up to the now bright window, where Abby saw two women smiling back.

A rush of excitement coursed through her body. "Don't stop." Without a conscious thought, her body's need was beyond any shyness. Having Victoria take her was the only thing that mattered and having that happen as others witnessed her surrender was—just—FUCK.

For a moment, Victoria's hand went lower, gliding over her belly button and lifting the very top of the silk panties. Abby's legs widened in anticipation. This was everything she wanted, right here, right now. She was going to be Victoria's...

And then she wasn't.

Victoria pulled back, placing a delicate kiss on her cheek. "We should talk over dinner."

Abby tried to hold back a whimper. The frustration was so overwhelming that tears pricked her eyes.

"Let me help you up." Victoria held out her hand and when Abby grasped it, she pulled the younger woman to her feet. "I'll introduce to Alison. You can tell her how much you appreciate her creations."

Abby nodded. She didn't want to appear like some petulant two-year-old or, even worse, a surly teenager. Christ, imagine if she acted like the angst-ridden teenager Victoria remembered from all those years ago. The irony of being unable to get laid as a mature woman, because of a fourteen-year-old's crush, was soul destroying. With a deep breath, she swallowed down her arousal and put on her most demure smile.

"Dinner would be good."

"Good. That was what I needed to hear." There wasn't a smugness to Victoria's reply, but Abby couldn't shake the feeling she was undergoing a series of tests and the outcome evaluated.

Damn. No matter how hard she tried, she was never any good at passing exams and practicals were even more daunting.

CHAPTER TEN

Alison's perpetual grin after having caught Victoria with Abby in the morning had been downright irritating. Thankfully, the morning's impromptu meeting had kept all three of them busy, so she hadn't had to worry about them interfering with Abby, or the shoot. The way Mhairi was so fiercely protective of Alison often bordered on scary. But Alison had been so charmed by Abby's complimentary response to her creativity that she'd won both of them over.

Intelligent, charming, funny, sexy and unafraid to share every aspect of who she was... Abby Mason on the face of it was everything that Victoria Fraser had ever wanted in a woman; in a sub. But she wasn't naïve enough to believe that after such a short amount of time, they knew enough to know they were a match.

It would be wrong to take another step without having some very honest communication. Hell, the woman had barely tickled around the edges of the world Victoria inhabited, albeit, as Alison constantly reminded her, she was more of a green card holder than a bona fide citizen.

Once Alison and Mhairi had left, and Abby had

wrapped up for the day, then she'd talk to her. Ask her to dinner. The rush of the morning's excitement would have worn off. They'd be able to have a less charged conversation. In her head, it all made sense. Perhaps when they'd spoken about the realities of exactly what a relationship would entail, that would be enough to stop the whole thing in its tracks. Maybe Abby didn't want a relationship. Now there was a thought. Perhaps she wanted nothing more than some no-ties exploration. If that was the case, then there was nothing more to talk about.

Placing the hurriedly put together plate of sandwiches on a tray, along with a large flask of coffee, she made her way back to the studio. The small kitchen within the studio had never been stocked, nor would it be. Not by them, at least. If guests wanted to use the facilities, then they could, but that would be their prerogative. Food kinks weren't her thing. At least that was a soft limit, although after seeing up close what Mhairi could do with an entire uncut cabbage had put Victoria off sauerkraut for life.

With Alison's cross submerged back into the basement, and the rug and furniture back in place, she found all three of them sitting, chatting.

"We were just telling Abby about the new Nuru massage range we're having produced." Alison crossed her lithe legs and placed a hand on Mhairi's knee. "It's a little tame for us, but we think it'll be a good seller. You haven't booked anyone to shoot the video for that yet, have you?" Alison's question was to Victoria.

Victoria felt her jaw clench. She had to put a stop to this before it started.

"No, but cheap videographers for that sort of thing are two a penny. We could probably shoot something like that ourselves if we had the inclination. Anyway, it isn't due for weeks yet." She smiled and placed the refreshments on the small coffee table in front of them. "Did Abby tell you she graduated from ECA too?"

"No, she didn't. I'd assume Photography? Would that be right?"

Victoria said a small silent hallelujah, delighted that Alison had taken the bait. As Abby and Alison talked about professors and artists, Victoria relaxed, choosing to sit next to Abby. Given the younger woman sat opposite her business partner and business partner's mistress, she thought it might make Abby feel a little less exposed.

Victoria studied her ex. Her hair was long, but pulled back with a clip. She'd talked about getting it cut into a shorter, more manageable style at one point, so it worked for her love of starting the day with a swim. But Mhairi liked Alison's long hair. Alison stopped swimming.

A wide black leather collar circled her neck beneath the long locks. It reminded Victoria of the disembodied Girl's World head she'd owned as a child. The model her parents had given her, had the faint, dazed look she'd subsequently seen on women portraying crack heads in CSI. Their make-up suggested she wasn't the only one who had learned the art of how to apply lipstick courtesy of Palitoy. The toy had an internal cog that shortened or lengthened the hair. If Alison had a cog, it was Mhairi's hand that was doing the winding.

When Abby so openly told them about her teenage crush on her sister's music teacher, who just happened to be Victoria, she was surprised at how warmly the words touched her. When the beautiful younger woman laughed and placed a hand on her knee, the feeling grew into something altogether more physical.

And then as she watched Alison and Abby banter back

and forth, oblivious to Mhairi's constant scrutiny, an old familiar doubt crept back in. What if she wasn't enough? What if Abby was more like Alison than either of them realised? She leaned back, crossing her legs and drawing her knee free of Abby's hand.

This, whatever this was, needed to be nipped in the bud, she decided.

Eventually, Mhairi grew bored with their chatter and, with a simple nod, indicated it was time to leave. It was a discrete, subtle gesture, and most people would have missed it entirely. But Victoria didn't.

Alison smoothed down her grey pencil skirt, and, thanking Victoria for lunch, stood, before turning to Mhairi, saying, "I need to get back. You don't mind, do you babes?"

It was such a small thing, but such a huge issue at the same time. Alison refused to acknowledge it, but that didn't stop Victoria from seeing it. It was one thing being a mistress in the bedroom, but another when that power play inhabited other areas of life, including who you should or shouldn't socialise with and for how long.

That was not okay.

No matter how hard Victoria tried, and she did, it was hard to hide her anger that grew from witnessing such coercive behaviour. Mhairi just stared back with equally obvious disdain. Grabbing her jacket from the back of the seat, she turned to Abby and said, "Abby, it was a pleasure to meet you. You must come over for dinner. Just the three of us. I think you might find our company a little more..." she paused, looking from Abby to Victoria and back again, "A little more satisfying." She wore a smug smile that fitted her even more tightly than the long wool coat Alison slid over her chubby arms.

Victoria felt a hot flare of anger shoot through her body,

but she wouldn't give Mhairi the satisfaction of seeing it on her face. Placing a hand on the small of Abby's back, she simply said, "At least Abby has the option to choose who she has dinner with."

Alison flashed a quick apologetic glance before grabbing their briefcases and striding ahead to open the door. Perhaps there were tiny cracks appearing in their relationship. Victoria knew Alison deserved better, and one day she hoped Alison would know that too.

———

After they had left, Victoria cleared away the plates and went through to find Abby. The young woman was dismantling the second of the two soft boxes used for the day's shoot. Victoria studied her methodically packing everything away. She seemed lost in thought or perhaps just deep in concentration. When Abby realised she was being watched, she jumped, one hand grabbing towards her chest.

"Oh," she gasped, her pitch high. "I didn't see you. I'm sorry." She seemed nervous and faltered for a moment before turning her attention to the Velcro which held the white diffusing panel to the soft box. A loud rip filled the air but in mid tear Abby stopped. Her shoulders slumped. "Look I'm sorry. I was so out of order this morning. I don't even know where to start. I'm not normally that—I don't know? Forward? I embarrassed you in front of your friends, made you feel awkward—" She shrugged, turning her eyes towards the ceiling and Victoria knew instantly what was happening. Abby was about to cry.

Shit. She had to do something, and she couldn't do it from ten feet away. Closing the distance between them, she reached out and took the half-collapsed frame from Abby's hands, letting it fall onto the floor. Taking her into her arms, she held her tight.

"You did nothing wrong," she whispered, and she meant it. Toying and teasing, building Abby's desire, had been her doing. The truth was, she had wanted Abby as much as Abby wanted her. She'd wanted her last night, too. Standing in front of her bedroom door, hearing the need in her moans, the hunger as she called Victoria's name. It was so beautifully painful, if not a little sad.

Was it just the torture of denial she was after, or was it something altogether more basic? Was she, the great Victoria Fraser scared? Scared of being hurt. Scared of not being enough. Scared that someone else could so easily swoop down and take what she loved. Again.

Abby's tears felt warm against her neck and she held her tight until she grew quiet. As Victoria loosened the embrace, Abby tilted her head up. Their lips were so close, barely a whisper between them. Neither moved. Victoria's heart pounded in her chest. She knew exactly what she wanted. To lean in and kiss Abby deeply. To allow their passion to build until neither could hold back any longer. Then she'd pin Abby against the wall, pull off her sweats and slide deep inside. But just because she wanted it, didn't mean it was what she should do.

"May I kiss you?" Abby sounded hesitant, fearful of rejection.

Victoria looked deep into her rich brown eyes, "I am going to grant you one kiss and then we're going to go back to the house, where you're going to gather all your things and go home."

"But—" The look of distress on Abby's face sent a shot of pain through Victoria's heart.

"No." Victoria shook her head firmly and placed one

finger over Abby's lips. "If you want me to take you to dinner tonight, then you need to go home and change." She smiled, wiped a tear from Abby's cheek, and then leant in to give her the sweetest kiss. Abby melted in her arms.

I'm going to do this the right way, Victoria thought, and deepened their kiss.

CHAPTER ELEVEN

At exactly 8 pm, the buzzer, it was actually a doorbell, but it literally buzzed, announced Victoria's arrival. Boy, she's punctual, thought Abby, who'd only just slipped into her clothes. Her hair was still wrapped in a towel. Sliding back the bolt, then turning the yale, she pulled open the heavy wooden door to welcome her guest. Abby's jaw hit the ground with a thud, not to mention a generous amount of drool. Standing in front of her, dressed in a short dark green above the knee number, topped with a long line military style jacket and knee-length boots, was Victoria. Beautiful loose auburn waves fell gently onto gold brocade detail.

"Are you going to invite me in?" Victoria asked with a raised eyebrow.

After several seconds, Abby regained consciousness.

"Yes. Come in. Sorry about the mess. I didn't have time to tidy *and* get myself ready, so I had to choose." She offered an open gesture towards her body, then her hair. "I won."

"So I see." Victoria let her gaze linger over the sleeveless sage coloured mini dress Abby had chosen. "I've a car waiting...have you still to do something with your hair?"

Abby whipped off the towel, bent over to expose a tiny tattoo at the nape of her neck, shook her hair, then roughly scrunched her fingers through it and said, "Ready." With a beaming smile.

The car was waiting, and Abby could feel her excitement build as the driver held the door open so she could slide into the leather backseat. Victoria hadn't told her where they were going or what to expect, and she hadn't asked. The mix of uncertainty and anticipation was arousing. The Mercedes glided away from her street and headed towards the old town. When she snatched a shy look at Victoria, she caught her staring back.

"What are you thinking?" The warmth of Victoria's fingers wrapped around her hand. It was a reassuring gesture telling Abby that there was nothing she couldn't say. Well, at least that's what Abby thought, given the kindness Victoria had shown her.

"That not knowing what's about to happen is kind of hot."

"Good," was all Victoria said. She let go of Abby's hand and patted it gently before turning her attention to the thrum of the city dancing past the side window. Ten minutes later, their car turned onto the castle esplanade and pulled up in front of the stone entrance of Advocates Close.

Abby knew the address. If they headed into the close, they'd come to The Monastery. Katie had always promised to take her there, but never did. In fairness, she'd never taken Katie there either, so she couldn't complain. Not really.

The Monastery in Edinburgh was an institution. Just say the name to any local and it resulted in an impressive eyebrow raise. It wasn't cheap, in fact, it was expensive, at least by Abby's standard. But by all accounts, it was fine dining at its best.

The driver opened Victoria's door first, and she twisted, lowered her feet to the cobbled stone and rose in one effortless movement. Abby hauled her ass across the back seat and followed in Victoria's wake. She too swung out her legs out, but with far less elegance, just as the driver opened the door next to where she had been sitting. She gave him a shrug. Well, that's the first etiquette test blown. She rewarded herself with an internal eye roll.

The two-inch heels she'd grabbed from the depths of her closet felt unsteady against the street's slippery surface. When she made it to the entrance without falling on her ass, she offered up a silent thank you. To whom she wasn't sure, but that didn't matter. To her surprise, the driver had followed them in and placed a large overnight bag at Victoria's feet. He nodded, asked if there was anything more and when she said 'No' he wished them both a pleasant evening and left.

"Are you staying here?" she asked.

Victoria smiled, but before she could answer, the young woman in the tailored black suit who was assisting them, spoke. "Ms. Fraser, we have the Sempill suite ready for you. I'll have someone take up your bags. Would you like to freshen up or go straight through to your private room for dinner?"

Holy shit. Abby tried to look casual and nonchalant, but she was pretty sure she wasn't pulling it off. There was a reason she wasn't a professional poker player.

"We'll have dinner, then retire. Thank you."

The word 'we'll' sent a flutter of excitement through Abby's stomach. "Be cool," she told herself, but really, she wanted to fist pump the air. She didn't. Obviously. Well, not really. There was just a small triumphant fist clench at her side as they walked through to dinner. The sheer opulence of the baroque oak panels and the deep red leather seating of the private dining room took her breath away.

"I pulled in favour or two and they agreed to open the private room for us at short notice," Victoria said.

A waiter pulled out a full backed leather studded chair for Victoria and Abby slid onto the long leather benched seat opposite. He seemed to know Victoria, as he confirmed her usual wine had been allowed to breathe for the specified time. Just as she liked it.

How often did you have to go somewhere for them to know your ideal wine breathing time? And who had a specified amount of time for wine to breathe? She might well be a heathen, but Abby's time to let a bottle of red settle, from opening to drinking, was about three seconds.

Their first course was oysters, followed by lemon sole. Abby had been happy for Victoria to order as she obviously knew the menu well, almost as well as Abby knew the weekly Uber Eats sushi deals. Victoria asked about Katie. How long had she lived in her apartment? Why she kept accepting wedding assignments if her heart wasn't in it?

The answer had been simple. Fifty per cent of her sizable inheritance, courtesy of her grandparents, went with Katie as part of the divorce settlement. Whilst Abby was far from broke, buying wine old enough that it needed to catch its breath, wasn't an everyday occurrence. Victoria took Abby's teasing in good humour, and she'd gotten to hear that laugh again. If Carlsberg did laughter...

It was during the main course that Abby had summoned up the courage to ask her burning question.

"So, why are you single?"

It was a question that occurred to her on more than six

occasions during the last two days and she hadn't managed to fathom a plausible explanation. Victoria was hot, funny, intelligent and had more integrity than almost anyone Abby had ever met, and hot, too. Had she thought 'hot' twice? If she had, doubly hot worked.

Victoria paused, taking a moment to think before offering an answer.

"I don't play games with people. Or have quick flings. Plus, I have very exacting standards." She smiled and then her face grew serious. "Sex should involve a strong emotional connection, especially when it involves an exchange of power. No matter how badly I wanted to touch you today, and I did, I really did. I couldn't. That's how people get hurt, and I'd never forgive myself if I hurt you."

Victoria's eyes met Abby's, and then the redhead reached across the table and took her hand. "Alison thinks I'm too soft. I disagree. I learned a lot from that relationship, but the greatest lesson was how important it is to never sacrifice your self-esteem. There have been a few women since Alison, but I've no desire to break down brattish behaviour, nor waste time with someone who simply does what they're told without engaging emotionally. Neither scenario offers me what I want—or need."

"What do you need?" Abby asked.

"Connection. But I've never found anyone that I get that rush with. That connection." Victoria picked up her wine glass with her free hand and stared. She seemed to be weighing something up and then gave an 'oh, fuck it,' sigh before continuing. "Until now."

Abby brushed her fingertips across Victoria's palm, just as Victoria had done to hers before. "I feel it too. And if we need to talk about limits and safe words before, you'll allow me to show you how I feel, can we please do that now? Or else I think I might—combust."

Victoria gave a hearty laugh, and right there, in that moment Abby knew. She just knew.

"We've already discussed my *many* hard limits, but you need you to know if we do this; I'm in control. You do exactly as I say. I'll always check in with you first, to make sure we agree on what is and isn't in play and that's for both of us. You need to feel safe and to trust me, and that takes time, but Abby I'm as eager as you, so... My safe word is wasabi, now you need to choose one."

"Fray Bentos," Abby said with a flourish.

"Fray Bentos? I won't ask, although I feel kind of relieved that it's not something you'd naturally say during sex. Now tell me about your limits. You've seen enough over the last couple of days to have some definite hard limits."

"I want to take it slow, explore a bit maybe. I'm not sure I'll ever want you to put me in a cage or stocks and the knife play thing is like a huge NO! And I'm not good with serious pain..." Abby paused and leant coyly towards Victoria. "But you looked so hot with that whip today—I might want to try that. But not too hard. At least not to start with?" Abby winced.

Victoria let out a small, kind laugh, as if understanding Abby's caution. She seemed to approve. "What if we try green, amber, red? If you want more, we are green all the way, ease off a little if you say amber and if we ever end up in the red, then it's straight to Fray Bentos. You say the word and that sets the pace. Would that work?"

"Yeah. I think it would. And Victoria?" Abby paused. "Thank you."

There were so many things she wanted to say, so much

she wanted to know but she held it all back. All except one question.

"I've just one more question. If that's okay?" She waited until Victoria nodded. "May I call you mistress?"

Victoria's eyes darkened; her pupils huge. Abby felt a bolt of electricity rip through her body and then she got her answer, but it wasn't what she expected.

"Tonight, you'll call me Ms. Fraser. The right to call me your mistress has to be earned."

The waiter discreetly appeared and, with Victoria's blessing, cleared away the residue of their mains. As if sensing the time was right, Victoria took control.

"I think we'll take a few moments, if you don't mind. I'll call you when I need you."

The waiter nodded, reversing out of the room, plates in hand, and pulled the large oak door firmly closed behind him.

Victoria levelled her gaze on Abby and stared. "Green, Amber and Fray Bentos. Do you have any questions?"

Abby swallowed, lowering her eyes as she felt her body respond to the appearance of Ms. Fraser. This was everything she wanted and more. "Green, Amber and Fray Bentos. No. No questions. I'm ready Ms. Fraser."

CHAPTER TWELVE

The sound of wood scraping across the floor filled the room as Victoria pushed back her chair from the table.

"Come here and don't speak unless I allow you to."

Abby slid out from behind the table and moved to stand in front of Victoria. The pounding of her heart reverberated through her body, echoing the need in her core.

"We need to work on your control, don't we?"

Abby faltered. Should she speak? Answer the question?

"Abby. Answer me."

"Yes, Ms. Fraser. We do."

"You come when I give you permission, and not before. I'm going to teach you that the best things are worth waiting for." Victoria opened her legs wide, and the hem of her short dress rode up to reveal her lack of underwear.

Abby's breath hitched. Ms. Fraser was wet. Very, very wet. Abby stared down as her beautiful Ms. Fraser glinted in the low light of the room.

Fuck, they were in a public place.

That thought notched up the voltage of her anticipation

with remarkable speed and her body twitched repeatedly. Would Ms. Fraser let Abby touch her?

"Take your dress off." Victoria watched Abby pull the dress she was wearing up and over her head. Ivory satin bra and panties were all that now covered the younger woman's body. "Now touch yourself."

Abby slid her hand inside her panties. Her fingers slid between her folds. Fuck, she was already so wet. A small shudder rolled through her body as a fingers ran down each side of her clit. She repeated the same action two, three times and her eyes fluttered closed.

"Open your eyes, Abby, and look at me."

Abby forced herself back into the room. Ms. Fraser was still facing her, her legs still wide open, her centre even wetter than before. *Jesus,* thought Abby, *I need to come."*

"Show me how much you want me to be your mistress, Abby. Keep looking at me, keep touching yourself, but don't you dare come. Do you want me to be your mistress, Abby?" Ms. Fraser's tone was harsher, bolder and her volume increasing.

Her voice; their unbroken eye contact; the public space; all added to the throng of Abby's arousal, but she didn't stop. The low rumble of an impending orgasm rolled through her centre. Her thighs shook, but still she didn't stop. This couldn't end here, staring into the beautiful green eyes of the one woman she had always wanted. Always adored. Please, God, no. The prickle of tears smarted in her eyes. Emotion tingled the end of her nose. She knew within a matter of seconds it would all be over.

"Stop." Victoria ordered.

Abby stilled her hand, but her body shuddered. She wanted to explode.

"Breath, Abby." This time Victoria's voice was softer. Exactly as it had been before.

"I'm sorry, Ms. Fraser." Abby's bottom lip quivered, emotion after emotion colliding as she desperately tried to keep it together.

"You have nothing to be sorry about. You did what I asked, and that was what I wanted. Now I want you to slip your panties off and sit on my lap."

Abby hesitated. If she had to touch herself again, her clit was so swollen she'd come within seconds.

"Now, Abby. I need you to trust me. Listen, and do what I say. Do you understand?" The edge to Ms. Fraser's tone let Abby know she didn't enjoy having to give an instruction more than once and, if nothing else, Abby was a fast learner.

With her panties discarded, she straddled Ms. Fraser's wide open legs. Their wetness so close Abby could feel Ms. Fraser's heat. Her breath caught as the hem of the older woman's dress glanced over her throbbing clit. But that was nothing to the agonising rise in tempo she felt as a hand pushed between their bodies, over her clit and rubbed over the length of her entrance.

"Abby, you've done excellent work. Now again, I don't want you to come. Do you understand?"

"Yes, Ms. Fraser." Abby felt two fingers slip deep inside, the base of a thumb rubbing over her clit. The rapid tingle of orgasm rose inside. There was no way she could stop what had started. Not now. A strangled groan escaped from her chest, and then she was empty. Ms Fraser had withdrawn her hand, leaving Abby still teetering on the very edge of climax.

"Get dressed, Abby." Victoria's hands lifted Abby's body up onto shaky legs and it was then Abby saw the wetness on Ms. Fraser's seat, beneath her beautiful gleaming centre.

Abby hadn't climaxed, but Ms Fraser...?

Victoria took a tissue from her bag, and regained her own composure as Abby dressed.

"You impressed me, Abby. I hadn't expected you to take instruction quite so well, and you were very—present." Ms. Fraser picked up her bag and turned to a fully clothed Abby, and said, "I think we'll have dessert in the suite if you're agreeable?"

Abby nodded. Need thrummed through her body, making it difficult to talk, and the thought of having to walk past other guests in her current state felt a little daunting. But if it meant she could be with Ms. Fraser, then it was a small price to pay.

CHAPTER THIRTEEN

Thankfully, the Sempill Suite was only one floor up, and it didn't disappoint. Gothic opulence surrounded them and when Abby was taken by the hand and led to the bottom of the four-poster bed, her eyes widened. This really was the stuff of fantasies.

The brief, sharp hissing of a zip ripping open made Abby turn. Victoria was very much still Ms. Fraser, and in her hand was a length of soft white rope.

"Remove your clothes, Abby." Her eyes had darkened considerably and Abby stripped.

Ms. Fraser kissed her deeply and pushed her back onto the bed. Without being told, Abby spread arms wide. The warm body of the woman she so desperately wanted to be her mistress climbed the full length of her body.

"Green. Amber. Fray Bentos. I can't believe I have to keep saying Fray Bentos. But anyway, are we good?"

Abby giggled. "Yes, Ms. Fraser, we're all good." Directly above Abby's face was the beautiful Ms. Fraser, straddling her shoulders. Abby inhaled deeply. Had she been with anyone else, it would have been the most natural thing in the world to reach up and grab her hips so she could pull the woman into her mouth. But not here.

The pressure of soft white ropes being secured around her left wrist made her pulse race. It was secure, but not too tight. One wrist, then the other. Ms. Fraser gave them a tug and when she seemed satisfied, they were good and tight between bedpost and wrist; she turned her attention back to a very excited Abby.

Lowered herself to within an inch of Abby's mouth, Ms. Fraser moved her hips in tiny circles so she was almost touching the younger woman but not quite.

"Only when I'm your mistress."

Abby groaned, frustration causing her body to buck.

"Don't disappoint me now. Not when you are so close." Victoria slipped a blindfold over Abby's eyes, stroked her cheek and asked, "Tell me where we are, Abby?"

"Green. Flashing like neon green!"

Victoria laughed and Abby felt the other woman's weight slip from the bed. After some light shuffling, warm hands on the inside of her thighs spread her legs wide and high, exposing every part of her. She heard a short squirt, then the cold slickness of long, elegant fingers slid through over her core, easing and exploring. Teasing and filling and pushing and rubbing.

Abby groaned and bucked and pulled against her restraints in the darkness. There was no way of knowing what was coming. She was living in the sheer chaos of the moment with her entire trust placed in her glorious Ms. Fraser. It was the most free she had ever felt.

"Do you still want me to be your mistress?"

"God, yes, Ms. Fraser." Abby bucked and felt something hard rub against her raised centre. It wasn't fingers or a hand, but it felt good. Her hips bucked again, desperate to feel its resistance. "Please," she begged.

"Are you ready, Abby? Are you sure this is what you want because when I take you there is no going back. You will be mine."

There was no hesitation, no second guessing. Abby had never been so sure, so clear, about what she wanted. She wanted to belong to Victoria, in mind, body and spirit. To give herself without reserve.

"Please take me, Ms Fraser. I want to be yours."

The full length of the strap-on sunk into Abby's centre and she screamed, "Yes."

The restraints pulled her wrists tight and Ms. Fraser held her legs wide open, gripping each ankle as she expertly slid the dildo deep into Abby's core. The rhythm was slow and steady, never missing a beat.

From nowhere, Abby felt a rush and screamed, "Ms. Fraser, I'm going to come." Immediately, the length of the shaft slipped out and Abby released an agonising roar.

"I didn't give you permission to come. If you want to come, you have to ask." Then, just as quickly as she'd had withdrawn, she re-entered, harder and deeper. Ms. Fraser pulled Abby's legs up to rest on her shoulders and she pushed her entire weight forward, picking up the pace. There was no question about it Ms. Fraser was claiming Abby as her own.

Abby felt her everywhere. The connection she felt consumed her. Within minutes, the tingle of orgasm was rising fast.

"Ms. Fraser, please can I come. Please." Her voice was thick with frustration, desperate for permission.

"I'm your mistress Abby. Address me correctly and ask again."

Hearing her mistress claim her nearly toppled her over the edge, but with her last ounce of control, she asked. "Mistress, please, can I come for you?"

"Come for me, Abby. Come for me."

They were the same words she'd heard before. It hadn't been a dream. Her mistress had been there.

As the white heat of orgasm ripped through her body, Abby surrendered to belong entirely to her mistress.

———

Abby lay curled into Victoria's body. Her mistress's scent, her touch, her care all around her; it felt so surreal yet so utterly real at the same time. Her mistress. She wanted to giggle with happiness. They had lain in the same position all night and Abby never wanted to move from this spot. No one had ever made her feel the way she had last night. It had been so—intimate, so sensual. Sure, she had been intimate with other women, even a few men when she was much younger, but last night with Victoria, was—it was on a different level.

Victoria shifted, tightening her arm and pulling Abby's body closer still. With the lightest touch, she followed the curve of her lover's skin. This was her mistress's arm. The breath that tickled the sensitive skin on the back of her neck belonged to her mistress. Would she ever tire of saying that word? Right now, lying in a bloody great four-poster bed, in her mistress's arms—IN HER MISTRESS'S ARMS—she wanted to kick her legs in delight. She felt so damned happy.

"What are you thinking about?" Victoria murmured softly in her ear.

"How happy I feel." Abby rolled over to face Victoria,

her smile stretching from ear to ear. "You haven't changed your mind, have you?"

"About what?" Victoria opened one eye and squinted at her.

"About being my mistress? About teaching me—stuff." Abby snuggled her head into the pillow.

Victoria blinked and opened both eyes so she could focus on Abby. "No. I told you I don't play games with people, especially not when it comes to relationships. And I don't act in the heat of the moment. I decide what I want and then I let it play out. If it's right, it works and if it doesn't, it wasn't mine to have. Why? Are you having second thoughts?" She pushed herself up onto one elbow, suddenly awake.

"Do I look like a woman that's having second thoughts?" Abby asked before dropping her hand beneath the bedsheets and tracing the toned curves of Victoria's body.

"You look like a woman that wants to take whatever I decide to give her." Victoria's smile grew, and then she leant forward and kissed Abby's nose. "But baby steps, Abby. I won't give you more than you can handle."

"I know. I trust you." Then a grin spread across her face. "Last night when you were—tying my wrists," Abby said, her face flushing with the memory, "I wanted to put my mouth on you and you said—"

Victoria stopped her with a single finger to her lips. The intensity which had filled her mistress's eyes was back.

"Oh, I know what I said, my little meat pie. The question is, have you earned enough privileges?"

"Mistress, if you tell me how, I'll gladly do whatever you ask of me." Abby meant every single word that came out of her mouth. The flecks of emerald in Victoria's irises seemed to dance in delight at what she was hearing.

"The answer is simple." She let out a long, amused sigh. While she might have tried to appear indifferent to Abby's interest, the slightest upturn at the corners of her mouth said otherwise. "You'll earn them through devotion and obedience. I have such plans for you. You have no idea."

Victoria traced a line from Abby's collarbone to her breast, carefully sketching the beautiful circle of pink surrounding her erect nipple. "You can start by removing these covers. I want you face down on the bed." Then, pushing back a wave of hair from Abby's face, she whispered in her ear. "By the time I have finished with you today, you'll not have enough energy to walk, never mind think about think about anything else."

The wicked grin that accompanied Victoria's promise sent a jolt of desire through Abby so strong she was up throwing a mountain of cushions, pillows and linen from the bed. It was like a Liberty volcano of soft furnishings.

There was nothing she wouldn't do for her mistress... within limits.

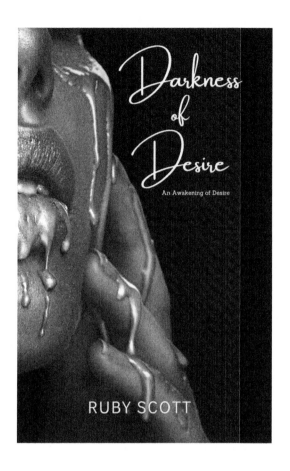

Keep reading about Abby and Victoria's story
in the sequel, "Darkness of Desire"

Out 7th Nov.

Your Words

are as important to an author

as an author's words

are to you.

(CLICK HERE)

Please leave me a review

Love Ruby x

Oh wait, before you go!

I hope you enjoyed getting this book

Subscribe to my newsletter and I'll send you a free sapphic romance

please sign up to my newsletter

ABOUT RUBY SCOTT

Ruby Scott lives in a quiet village nestled in the Scottish hills with her wife Angie and their furry little girl, Bailey. As an avid reader of she got up one day, had an extra cup of coffee, and thought, I'm going to write a book.

It's amazing where an extra cup of coffee can take you. Endless curiosity combined with a love of traveling and books, Ruby is never without adventure.

It's an adventure everyone is welcome to join.

Awakening of Desires

May I Call You Mistress?

Darkness Of Desire

City General: Medic 1 Series

Hot Response

Open Heart

Love Trauma

Diagnosis Love

Trails of the Heart

Healing of the Heart

Stronger You Series

Inside Fighter

Seconds Out

On The Ropes

Evergreen Series

Evergreen

The Velvet Storm Series

The Stranger Within Me

Strangely Familiar

RUBY SCOTT AKA FRANKIE DUNCAN

If you like a romantic comedy you may like these novels by
the same author.

First Comes Love

Love In Action

Her Christmas Escape

Ruby Scott

www.rubyscott.com

Printed in Great Britain
by Amazon